This book was created for you by:

Illustrator - Author and Victoria Harwood

Igor Kirko - Editor

Leslie Harwood - Translator

This book is your new adventure with amazing discoveries!

You will read a story about a young island, born in the middle of a far away ocean.
The island turns out to be a real hero!

It learns about what it is, manages to survive a storm, raises a friend and becomes a good protector for other creatures, on the island and in the salty ocean.

There is a tiny island that lives in the middle of a large ocean.
Yes, islands live too, they can even celebrate their birthdays!

This little island has a name, its name is Ploof...
I'm sure you are wondering how it got its odd name?
I'll explain.

The island didn't know its name until the salty sea wind noticed the new little island and heard the waves splashing against the sand on its shore:

Shhh...ploof...shhh...ploof.
That's why the sea wind decided to call it Ploof.

The sea wind liked the island and for its birthday, gave it a coconut.

As well as something you eat, a coconut is a seed.

But Ploof was still a very young island and didn't know that.

Ploof did not want the nut to roll back into the sea.
So Ploof asked two crabs that lived on this island to cover it with sand.

Little Ploof loved to be surrounded by the sea waves.

Under the water it played with the fish and watched the corals and undersea plants grow.

When Ploof was born, a long time ago, the days were sunny and the waves sparkled in the sun, making hissing sounds against the sand.

Ploof thought it would always be like that!

It's very heavy rain with strong winds. It gets dark because the sun is behind thick grey clouds and can be chilly too.

It also rumbles loudly and lights up everything around with lightning.

The little island was covered by huge waves again and again, and the rain poured down like a watering can from the sky.

Ploof was very worried, it tried its best to keep hold of his wonderful white sand, because under the sand funny little crabs lived!

Ploof also wanted to protect the fish under the water, giving them shelter in between the rocks nearby.

So the storm went on for two or three days, or maybe more...

Ploof did not know how to count, for it was an island, not a human.

Ploof was feeling tired from this storm and fell asleep.

Ploof slept for a long time probably several days.

When it woke up, the sun was shining and the gentle warm winds were back playing around it again.
Ploof was going to get a surprise.

At the place where the gift from the sea was hidden, there was now a tiny sprout.

The sprout already had two leaves which were reaching outwards and upwards towards the sun.

It was the storm rains that watered the sand with fresh water.

Water in the sea and oceans is very salty.

Plants and animals drink fresh water, not saltywater. So do you!

Ploof is very happy now, it has a real friend. It can take care of the young plant.

The little island understood that storms and thunder are not bad at all, they can be the start of something new.

The sprout soon began to grow into a tall coconut palm with long green leaves.
Even the crabs were happy to shelter under the palm's shade...

Thank you for reading this story about our little hero - the island called PlooF!

There is some truth in every fairytale!

I am sure that now you know more about the ocean's inhabitants.

Be brave, read more interesting stories and fairytales and magical doors to other adventures will start opening for you!

ISBN

Printed in Great Britain
by Amazon